MARGRET & H.A.REY'S
Curious George
in the Snow

Illustrated in the style of H. A. Rey by Vipah Interactive

Houghton Mifflin Company   Boston

Visit us at www.abdopublishing.com

Reinforced library bound edition published in 2008 by Spotlight, a division of ABDO Publishing Group, 8000 West 78th Street, Edina, Minnesota 55439. This edition was published by agreement with Houghton Mifflin. www.houghtonmifflinbooks.com

Based on the character of Curious George®, created by Margret and H. A. Rey. Illustrated by Vipah Interactive, Wellesley, Massachusetts: C. Becker, D. Fakkel, M. Jensen, S. SanGiacomo, C. Yu. For information about permission to reproduce selections from this book, write to Permissions, Houghton Mifflin Company, 215 Park Avenue South, New York, New York 10003.

Library of Congress Cataloging-in-Publication Data

Margret & H.A. Rey's Curious George / illustrated in the style of H.A. Rey by Vipah Interactive [et al].
    v. cm.
    Contents: Curious George and the dump truck -- Curious George and the firefighters -- Curious George and the hot air balloon -- Curious George feeds the animals -- Curious George goes camping -- Curious George goes to a movie -- Curious George in the snow -- Curious George makes pancakes -- Curious George takes a train -- Curious George visits the library -- Curious George's dream -- Curious George's first day of school.
    ISBN 978-1-59961-410-6 (Curious George and the dump truck) -- ISBN 978-1-59961-411-3 (Curious George and the firefighters) -- ISBN 978-1-59961-412-0 (Curious George and the hot air balloon) -- ISBN 978-1-59961-413-7 (Curious George feeds the animals) -- ISBN 978-1-59961-414-4 (Curious George goes camping) -- ISBN 978-1-59961-415-1 (Curious George goes to a movie) -- ISBN 978-1-59961-416-8 (Curious George in the snow) -- ISBN 978-1-59961-417-5 (Curious George makes pancakes) -- ISBN 978-1-59961-418-2 (Curious George takes a train) -- ISBN 978-1-59961-419-9 (Curious George visits the library) -- ISBN 978-1-59961-420-5 (Curious George's dream) -- ISBN 978-1-59961-421-2 (Curious George's first day of school)
    [1. Monkeys--Fiction.] I. Rey, Margret. II. Rey, H. A. (Hans Augusto), 1898-1977. III. Vipah Interactive. IV. Title: Margret and H.A. Rey's Curious George.
    PZ7.M33582 2008
    [E]--dc22   2007035446

This is George.

George was a good little monkey and always very curious.

One cold day George went to a winter sports competition with his friend, the man with the yellow hat. They were outside all morning and wanted to warm up with a hot drink.

At the ski lodge on top of the mountain, the man said, "George, why don't you wait at this table while I get some hot chocolate? I'll be right back, so don't get into any trouble."

George liked being on top of the mountain; there was so much to see! Why, there was something interesting.

George thought it looked like a spaceship.

He was curious. What was a spaceship doing on a mountain?

George forgot all about waiting for the hot chocolate...

and climbed in. A man in a racing suit saw him and said, "What are you doing in my sled?" He tried to stop George, but it was too late. The sled shot down the mountain—with George inside!

This is no spaceship, thought George. This is a rocket!

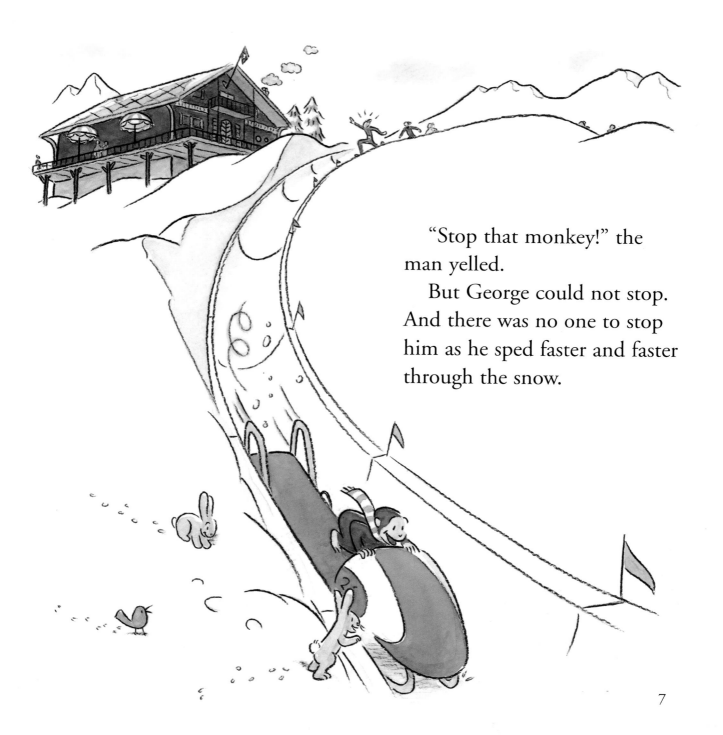

"Stop that monkey!" the man yelled.

But George could not stop. And there was no one to stop him as he sped faster and faster through the snow.

Suddenly the sled slipped
sideways — George didn't know
how to steer.

The sled swished through some trees

and whacked into a pole!

9

Luckily, George was not hurt, but this was not where he was supposed to be. Now how would he get up the mountain? George looked at the sled. It was stuck by the pole. He looked up the pole.

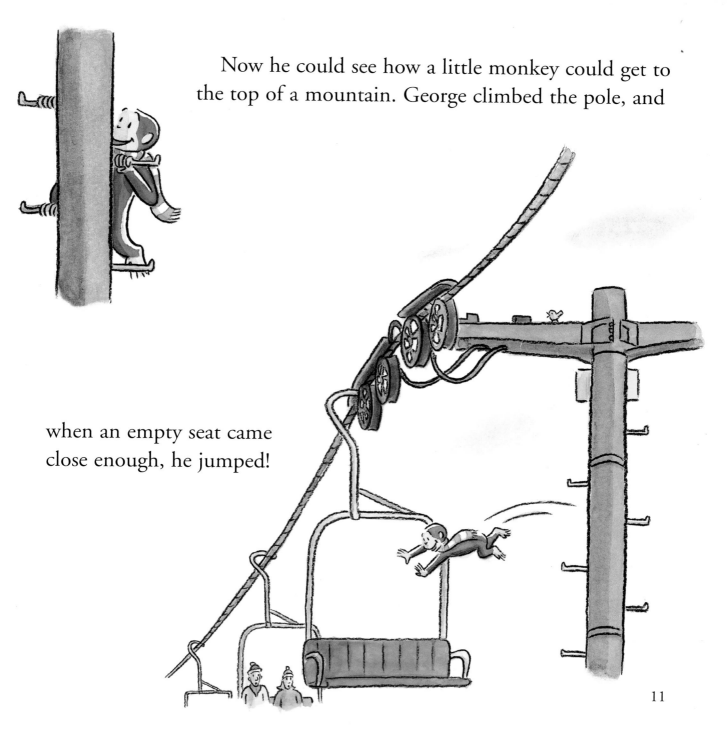

Now he could see how a little monkey could get to the top of a mountain. George climbed the pole, and

when an empty seat came close enough, he jumped!

11

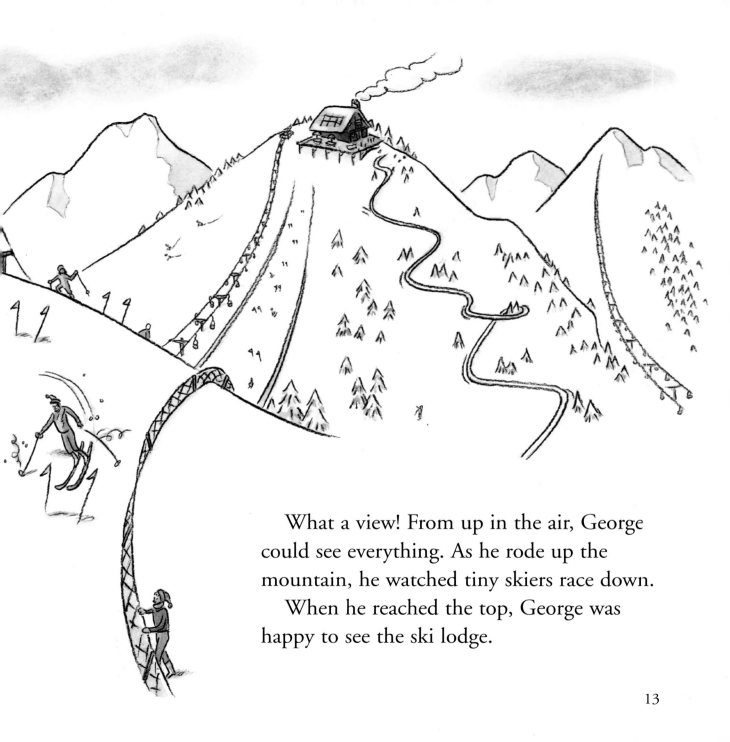

What a view! From up in the air, George could see everything. As he rode up the mountain, he watched tiny skiers race down.

When he reached the top, George was happy to see the ski lodge.

This was where he was supposed to be!

George found the table. But he couldn't find the man with the yellow hat.

Where could he be?

George looked down the mountain.

There was someone who looked like his friend! Maybe his friend was going down to get George. But how could George get down the mountain this time?

If only he had another sled . . .

Why, here was a
monkey-sized sled.

George took the sled down

and gave himself a push. The sled
was quick to pick up speed on the
steep mountain.

George zigged this way
and that way, then another
way altogether.

He flew over a hill

and landed on the raceway!
"It's a monkey!" yelled a boy,
and the crowd cheered.

"Look out, little monkey!"
someone yelled from the crowd.
    But George was going so fast
that the wind roared in his ears,
and he could not hear!

But George could see.
    He saw a skier right in
front of him.
    Could he stop?

No!

The crowd gasped as George crashed into the skier and flew up in the air. The skier went tumbling and his ski snapped right in half. When George came down...

he landed on the broken ski . . . and kept going!

The crowd was amazed. "What is he doing?" they asked. "Is he skiing? Is he sledding?"

"He's surfing in the snow!" said a boy.

George sailed down the mountain and came to a smooth stop.

What a show! The crowd cheered as George took a bow. No one had seen skiing like this before! When the skier arrived, everyone was glad to see that he was not hurt, and they cheered for him, too. Soon the man with the yellow hat arrived. He was glad to find George.

George was glad to finally find his friend. The man with the yellow hat made his way through the noisy crowd to apologize to the skier. "I'm sorry George caused so much trouble," he said.

"That's okay," said the skier. "I still have another race — and another pair of skis." Then he said, "That was some skiing, George!"

Later that day, the skier raced again — and won! It was a new record! The crowd went wild. They were still cheering when the skier found George at the finish line. "Thanks to you, George, this big crowd stayed to cheer me on," he said. "I couldn't have won without them — or you."

23

He lifted George to his shoulders and the crowd cheered once more for their favorite monkey skier, George.

The end.